OAK TREE TALES

Master Rabbit Leaves Home

Dorothea King

Master Rabbit was bored. So bored, in fact, that he couldn't even be bothered to do any of the things he liked best. Going fishing was too much of an effort because it meant digging for worms. Extending his burrow was out of the question as the wheel had fallen off his barrow months ago, and he couldn't be bothered to put another one on. It did cross his mind to go and find his friend, Barnaby the Hare, but he would want to play racing or something which took up a lot of energy.

"Perhaps I'll go and dig up some carrots," he thought lazily, but then decided against it when he remembered the handle on his spade needed replacing. Nevertheless the thought of food did keep drifting back and forth across his mind, especially when the smell of baking wafted through his window.

He took a big sniff. "Umm--mmm," he said to himself. "Must be Saturday. Mistress Hedgehog's baking day."

Being a cunning little rabbit he knew that Mistress Hedgehog wasn't likely to give him some of her cake without a reason, especially as he had annoyed her only yesterday by knocking her washing line over. No, he would definitely have to get in her good books again before she would let him sample any of her cakes.

Suddenly an idea came to him. "Flowers," he said. "What lady could resist a bunch of flowers?"

Whistling gaily he leapt out of bed, and after a quick wash and brush-up put on his best clothes, including a tie. "Just to impress her."

Outside in the clearing there were masses of wild
flowers, but he decided they were much too ordinary. "I
really need something a little different," he said thoughtfully, and then remembered where he had seen some
really beautiful flowers. "Of course," he grinned. "Why
didn't I think of it before?"

Quickly he hopped up Sir Squirrel's staircase and crept
around the tree to his greenhouse. Inside were masses of
the squirrel's prize blooms. He was a keen gardener and
always won first prize at the Squirrel Association Annual
Flower Show.

"He'll never miss them," said the rabbit, gathering a large bunch of assorted flowers.

Mistress Hedgehog was most surprised when she opened her door and found the rabbit on her doorstep.

"What have you been up to now?" she said suspiciously.

"Nothing," replied the rabbit in amazement.

"That's unusual," replied the hedgehog.

"Just thought you might like these," said the rabbit, and thrust the flowers forward.

"Why?"

The rabbit scratched his head thoughtfully. This idea was definitely not going according to plan.

"Because I broke your washing line yesterday."

"Well, in that case go and mend it," she said, and slammed the door in his face.

Master Rabbit, not to be put off, especially as the baking smelt so good, yelled back through the letter box:

"If I do will you give me one of your cakes?"

"No!" yelled back Mistress Hedgehog.

"Just a little one..."

By this time, Mistress Hedgehog was so agitated with the rabbit, that all she wanted was to be left alone to finish her baking.

"Yes, all right," she called back, even louder than before.

The rabbit was highly delighted. "The flowers did work after all," he said, and went off to fetch his toolbox and a length of rope.

It didn't take him long to make the new washing line and he was very pleased with himself when it was finished. "She'll be thrilled with it," he said to himself. "It's much better than the last one."

Knocking smartly on Mistress Hedgehog's door he went to collect his reward. "Think I'll choose an iced bun," he said. "Or maybe a slice of gingerbread. In fact she will probably give me both when she sees what a splendid job I've made of her washing line!"

Proudly he took Mistress Hedgehog out to show her his handiwork

...and was most amazed when she hit him over the head with a wet teacloth.

"You stupid little animal," she yelled. "How on earth do you expect me to hang my washing on that when it's halfway up the tree? I haven't got wings you know."

And with that she stamped into her house slamming the door behind her.

Master Rabbit was still standing there feeling most bewildered when a sudden gush of water from above took him completely by surprise and knocked him off his feet. Looking up he saw Sir Squirrel glaring down at him still holding an empty bucket.

"That's for stealing my flowers," he yelled.

"How did you know it was me?" said the rabbit in amazement.

"Who else would it have been?" shouted the squirrel, and stormed back into his house.

The rabbit wasn't bored anymore, he was just miserable and very uncomfortable. There he sat, hungry and wet, not knowing quite what to do next, when he heard Miss Mouse singing a merry little tune.

"At least somebody's happy," he said and, being in need of cheering up, went and knocked on her door.

He waited a few minutes but Miss Mouse was singing so loudly that she couldn't hear him, so he went inside.

Miss Mouse had only just finished washing her kitchen floor and was emptying her bucket when the rabbit appeared beside her. He was still dripping wet and his feet were now covered in mud.

She took one look at him and then at her floor, which was now covered in large muddy footprints.

"Look what you've done," she screamed. "My nice clean floor, now I've got to do it all again."

The rabbit very quickly got the feeling he wasn't welcome and without waiting to explain why he had come, rushed back outside leaving yet another set of muddy footprints.

Miserable, wet and hungry he slouched back to his burrow, and that was the last any one saw of him that day.

The following morning Mistress Hedgehog was having her breakfast when she suddenly realised that everything was very quiet. There was no banging coming from the rabbit's burrow and she couldn't even hear him talking to himself, which was most unusual.

"Expect he's still feeling miserable," she thought to herself as she cleared away the breakfast things. Now, in spite of the fact she was always having problems with the rabbit, Mistress Hedgehog quite liked him really and as the morning went by and she finished her chores she began to get a little concerned.

"I did treat him rather badly yesterday," she said. "Especially when he brought me flowers. Just to make up for it, I'll take him some of his favourite cakes."

She chose the best cakes she could find and bustled out to his burrow.

When she got there, she gave a gasp of surprise, and then a loud sob which brought the squirrel and Miss Mouse dashing out into the clearing.

Pinned to the rabbit's door was a large notice saying:

The animals didn't know what to do. Miss Mouse and Mistress Hedgehog were most upset and even Sir Squirrel mumbled, "Didn't realise I had upset the little fellow quite so much."

All that day, they searched and searched but there was no sign of the rabbit anywhere, and they were all convinced they would never see him again.

The rabbit, of course, was perfectly all right, and had found the ideal spot to build a new burrow. "It was time I moved out," he said. "At least I won't be bored now I have a new burrow to build."

Before he left home he had designed a complicated system of passages, shafts and tunnels which would give him a much larger house than before, and when he had finished it he could invite the others to stay.

He made such good progress the first day that by
evening the first room was complete.

The following morning he was up at the crack of dawn, ready to begin the first long tunnel. It was to be longer than any other tunnel he had ever made.

By mid-morning he was deep into the earth and was really excited with his new home. "Only a few more feet and the tunnel will be finished," he said as he took a mighty swing with his pickaxe.

Suddenly something grabbed the axe and the rabbit was pulled off his feet through the earth and into...

a mole's house.

The mole was extremely angry and started to chase the rabbit out of his house. Quick as a flash the rabbit dived down another tunnel with the mole close behind him.

He rounded a bend only to find himself at a kind of cross roads. He looked around frantically, which way could he take?

"Come back, you scoundrel!" he heard the mole shout.

"No fear!" said the rabbit and shot off to the right, running as fast as his feet could carry him.

The tunnel ended and he found himself surrounded by roots. Immediately he began to feel safer. "At least it's somewhere to hide," he panted, and went deeper and deeper into the roots.

So intent was he in getting away from the mole that he was quite unprepared for what happened next.

A large furry hand suddenly grabbed him from behind. "He's caught up with me," gasped the rabbit, thinking it must be the mole. But it wasn't, it was a very large ugly stoat...and a very unpleasant character he looked as well.

The rabbit's knees began to quiver, his teeth began to chatter and he felt dreadfully sick.

"Nice of you to pay me a visit," smiled the stoat, licking his lips.

"I w--w--was just p---assing through really," stuttered the rabbit. "Didn't mean to disturb you."

"You're not disturbing me at all. In fact I was just thinking to myself, wouldn't it be nice if a fat little rabbit paid me a visit."

"Oh, I haven't time to visit," said the rabbit weakly.

"Sure you have," grinned the stoat and with one tug pulled the rabbit into his smelly little house.

"The only problem is," the stoat said thoughtfully rubbing his chin, "I'm completely out of onions and herbs."

"Don't bother to get some for me," the rabbit assured him. "I never have liked onions."

The stoat seemed to think this was terribly funny, and was still laughing as he went out slamming the door shut behind him.

The rabbit was quite frantic. He could tell the stoat was up to no good and knew he had to make a fast escape.

He went around the room testing the walls with his paw and eventually found a place where the earth was soft and crumbly. Thankfully it was behind a large chair where the stoat, should he come back, would be less likely to see where the rabbit had dug himself out.

Rolling up his sleeves the rabbit began to burrow faster than he had ever done before. He didn't care where he came up as long as it was far away from the stoat and the mole.

Further and further he went into the earth until at last he was far enough away and could start going upwards.

Mistress Hedgehog was sitting by her fire, sipping a mug of hot chocolate when she saw the rug begin to move.

Up and up it went.

She rubbed her eyes in disbelief. It seemed to be rising from the floor.

"Ah---hh--!" she screamed, and dropped the mug on the floor.

The rug was standing in front of her - but it had two feet - furry feet - rabbit's feet!

Quickly she snatched the rug away...and there stood the rabbit.

"Just thought I'd pop in for a minute," he grinned weakly.

"You stupid little animal," Mistress Hedgehog gasped, and much to the rabbit's surprise gave him a big hug.

Obviously the others were all pleased to see him, and Mistress Hedgehog prepared a fantastic midnight feast of all the rabbit's favourite food.

"What made you decide to come back?" the animals asked.

"Oh there's no place like home sweet home," the rabbit replied.